In Business with Mallory

For everyone at Lerner—
You make the book business fun!
All my thanks,
—L. B. F.

For my daughter Miranda,
future businesswoman
—B. P.

In Business with Mallory

by Laurie Friedman

illustrations by Barbara Pollak

Carolrhoda Books, Inc. / Minneapolis

CONTENTS

A WORD FROM MALLORY

Have you ever wanted to buy something, but when you ask your parents, they say, "No"? So you say, "Pretty please, with sugar and cream on top!"

Then your parents say, "No! We are not buying that thing."

So you say, "Please, please, please buy that thing! I have to have that thing!" And just in case your parents don't get how important that thing is to you, you hug them and tell them you love them. Then you wait.

You wait for your parents to say, "Awww (fill in your name here), that is the sweetest thing we've ever heard. Of course we'll buy that (fill in the name of the thing you've been talking to them about here) for you."

But that's not what they say.

What they say is, "(put your name here and say it in a not-so-nice way), we will not buy that (say the name of the thing here like you're talking about a bad virus that's going around your school) for you."

And then they say they're through talking and no matter what you say, you're not getting what you want.

And that's when you get a feeling . . . an If-I'm-ever-going-to-get-what-I-want-I'm-going-to-have-to-find-a-way-to-get-it-myself feeling.

If that's something you've felt, then you and I have a lot in common. I'm Mallory McDonald, age just-turned nine, and that's exactly how I'm feeling.

The problem is . . . figuring out what to do about it.

THE PERFECT PURSE

"Max, out of the way! You're blocking *Fashion Fran!*"

I pick up my cat, Cheeseburger, and move from one end of the couch to the other. I want to see my favorite TV show, NOT my brother's back.

Max plops down on the couch where I was sitting. He picks up the remote and starts flipping through the channels.

"Hey! What are you doing?" I try to grab the remote out of his hands, but Max is too fast. He finds a baseball game and then shoves the remote under his seat cushion.

"Who wants to watch a dumb show about what to wear?"

"I do!"

I know Max is going to say, "*Too bad. I don't!*" But I don't wait for him to say it.

"MOM!" I yell. "I was watching *Fashion Fran* and Max changed the channel."

Mom walks into the family room. "Max, take turns. Let Mallory finish her show, then you can pick something you want to watch."

"She can watch whatever she wants," Max says like he was never planning to not let me watch my show. "I'm going outside."

I hate when Max acts like he wasn't doing something that he knows he was doing. I pick up the remote and switch back to Fran.

"Now, for the latest in rain gear," says Fran.

Just as Fran starts modeling a raincoat with matching boots and an umbrella, the phone rings. I pick up the receiver on the coffee table next to the couch before anybody else has a chance to. "Hey, hey, hey!" I say into the phone.

I wait for my lifelong best friend to say *hey, hey, hey* back, but it's not Mary Ann's voice on the other end.

"Hey Mal," says a boy's voice. "Want to meet me at the wish pond and we can go skateboarding?"

I love skateboarding with Joey. Ever since I moved to Wish Pond Road, he's been

a great next-door neighbor, a great skateboarding instructor, and a great friend, but I can't go skateboarding in the middle of my favorite show. "Another day," I tell Joey.

I hang up the phone. While Fran demonstrates how the raincoat can be worn on either side, the phone rings again. "What now?" I ask when I pick up the phone.

But this time, it isn't a boy's voice like I thought it would be.

"Hey, hey, hey!" says a voice on the other end. I grin into the receiver. It's Mary Ann! "Are you watching our favorite show?" she asks me.

Mary Ann and I made a pinkie swear a long time ago to never miss an episode of *Fashion Fran.* "What else would I be doing?" I ask.

Even though it was more fun watching *Fashion Fran* with Mary Ann before I moved to Fern Falls, we still like watching it together. I snuggle into the couch and hold the phone with one hand and Cheeseburger with the other.

Fashion Fran puts away her umbrella. "I'm saving this for a rainy day!" she says with a smile. Then she takes out a shiny purple box. "The next item I have to show you is very special." She opens the lid to the box and pulls out a purse.

"This is not just any purse," says Fashion Fran. "This is the Perfect Purse." She holds the purse up so it fills the TV screen.

"Cute, cute, cute!" gasps Mary Ann.

"So, so, so!" I gasp back. Mary Ann and I always like the same things.

Fran starts taking things out of the purple box.

"The Perfect Purse is perfect because it's not just *one* purse. The Perfect Purse comes with ten custom-designed covers in a variety of today's most

fashionable colors, patterns, and textures, including faux fur, leopard print, crushed velvet, sequins, a patriotic stars and stripes pattern, polka dots, and a lovely rainbow design," she says.

"There's even a waterproof cover for rainy days." Fran holds covers up to the TV screen so we can see them at home.

"I love the leopard print," says Mary Ann.

"So do I." The leopard print is definitely my favorite.

"But that's not all," Fashion Fran tells us. "The Perfect Purse also comes with a sparkly butterfly pin to dress up your purse for the most formal of affairs."

The TV shows a picture of Fran in a long red dress. She's carrying the Perfect Purse with the stars and stripes cover on it and the butterfly pinned to it.

"That was me at the Firecracker Ball on the 4th of July," Fran says, smiling.

"Wow," says Mary Ann. "Fran looked so pretty."

"You'll never need another purse if you have

the Perfect Purse," says Fran. She hugs hers to her chest. "Get yours while supplies last. They won't be around for long."

Fashion Fran waves. "That's it for today," she says. "See you tomorrow with more of the latest, greatest finds in the world of fashion." Fran blows a kiss.

I click off the TV. "What a great episode," I say.

"What a great purse," says Mary Ann. "I wish I had one."

"Yeah, me too."

Mary Ann sighs like it's really sad that we don't. Then she squeals into the phone. "Let's both get one! We'll have matching purses!"

I feel like a marching band just marched into my ear. "How are we going to do that?" I ask.

"Simple," says Mary Ann. "I'll ask my

mom to get me one. You ask your mom to get you one."

Mary Ann knows my mom well enough to know that she says *no* to a lot of things. "But what if my mom says *no*?"

"She won't say *no*," says Mary Ann. "Just tell her how perfect the Perfect Purse is and I know she'll get it for you."

I hope Mary Ann is right. I hope Mom will say yes.

"I can't believe I didn't think of this before," Mary Ann says in her marching band voice. "When my mom and I come to visit in two weeks, we can wear our matching purses. It will be fun, fun, fun!"

Mary Ann and her mom come to visit a lot now . . . now that her mom is dating Joey's dad. Even though I'm not sure I like that my old best friend's mom is dating my new best friend's dad, I do like that Mary

Ann comes to Fern Falls more often.

"It sounds like fun," I tell Mary Ann.

"And it will be. You get your mom to get you one. I'll get my mom to get me one. Having the Perfect Purse is all I can think about!" she says.

"Yeah," I tell Mary Ann. But when I hang up the phone, *having* the Perfect Purse isn't all I can think about. *Getting* the Perfect Purse is all I can think about.

I hope it will be as simple as Mary Ann says it will be.

MALL MADNESS

Mom pulls into a parking space at the mall. Our van looks like one tiny goldfish in a big aquarium filled with hundreds of goldfish. There are cars everywhere.

"I think everyone in Fern Falls decided to go shopping today," I say to Mom as we walk toward the mall.

Mom points to a sign hanging over the opening of the mall. "It's Mall Madness."

"Why would anybody get mad about

coming to the mall?" I ask.

Mom laughs as we walk into a department store. "This kind of madness doesn't mean people are angry. It means they're excited. There are a lot of sales going on, so people are excited to go shopping," she explains as we head up the escalator to the Girls' Department.

That makes sense to me. I hadn't thought of it before, but I'm mad too. Mad with excitement, but not to buy the underwear we came to buy. I'm excited to buy what I want, and what I want is the Perfect Purse.

I hope I can find what I'm looking for.

When we get to the Girls' Department, Mom starts looking through a pile of underwear. She holds up a pair in front of her for me to see.

But what I see behind Mom is much more

exciting than what's in front of her. It's the Perfect Purse! I didn't think something so perfect could be so easy to find.

I reach around Mom and pick up a purse off of the display. "It's the Perfect Purse!" I say, holding up the purse for Mom to see.

Mom laughs. "I'm sure it is the perfect purse, but these are the perfect underwear. Your size and on sale." Mom picks up a pink pair and a yellow pair.

I don't know how Mom can think about something as boring as underwear at a time like this.

"Mo-o-o-o-o-o-o-o-m! This *really* is the Perfect Purse." I hold it up so she can see what I already know. "Just look! This purse comes with ten covers." I show her the covers on the display. Then I read her the advertisement that is on the back of the box.

"The Perfect Purse comes with ten custom-designed covers in a variety of today's most fashionable colors, patterns, and textures, including faux fur, leopard print, crushed velvet, sequins, a patriotic stars and stripes pattern, polka dots, and a lovely rainbow design. There's even a waterproof cover for rainy days, and a sparkly butterfly pin to dress up your Perfect Purse for the most formal of affairs."

I start to read Mom the part of the ad that says if you buy the Perfect Purse you will never need another purse. But Mom stops me.

"Mallory, we came to buy underwear for you and cleats for Max, not a purse."

I give Mom an *I-want-the-purse-and-not-the-underwear* look. "Mary Ann and I made a promise. She promised her mom would get her one, and I promised you would get me one." I lay the purse gently in Mom's arms, like it's a baby kitten.

Mom looks at the purse in her arms, but not like it's a helpless little animal.

"Mallory, just because Mary Ann is getting it doesn't mean you're going to." Mom looks down at the price tag. "This is a very expensive purse." She pushes the price tag toward me so I can see too.

But I don't need to look to know that it

costs more than most purses. "It costs more than one purse," I tell Mom, "because it's like having ten purses."

Mom looks at me like that doesn't make any sense.

Even though math isn't my best subject, I try to explain. "If we bought ten purses, they would cost more than one purse, so we are actually saving money if we buy the Perfect Purse because it costs less than ten purses."

I wait for my explanation to sink in, but Mom shakes her head. She puts the purse back on the display, picks up an armload of underwear, and walks to the cash register.

I look at the Perfect Purse that Mom put back, and I think about Mary Ann. I bet right now she's at the mall with her mom, and I bet her mom's not buying underwear.

"C'mon, Mallory." Mom says my name in

a *follow-me-and-don't-ask-for-anything-else* look. We go back down the escalator and through the mall.

As we pass the fountain in the courtyard of the mall, I watch the shopping bag in Mom's hand swing back and forth. I can't help wishing that bag was filled with something besides underwear. I tap Mom on the shoulder. "May I please have a penny?"

Mom smiles and opens her purse. "I don't see why not." She hands me a penny.

I squeeze it in my hand and pretend like I'm at the wish pond at the end of my street. I do what I always do when I want something to happen. I make a wish.

I wish somehow, some way, I will get the Perfect Purse.

I throw my penny into the fountain and watch it sink to the bottom. I hope my wish

comes true. I follow Mom to the athletic store to get a pair of cleats for Max.

I'm quiet while Mom shops for Max. When she finishes, we walk back through the department store to go to our car. As we pass the escalator that leads up to the Girls' Department, I put my hand on Mom's arm to stop her.

I think about the penny I threw into the fountain. I think now is the time for my wish to come true.

"Mom." I try to keep my voice calm and talk to her the way grown-ups do when they really want other grown-ups to do something. "I know you already said *no*, but it would make me really happy if you would please buy the Perfect Purse for me."

I try to keep a pleasant look on my face while I wait for Mom's answer.

But I don't have to wait long. I look at

Mom's face, and it doesn't look nearly as pleasant as mine. Her voice doesn't sound calm either.

"Mallory, we are through talking about the Perfect Purse.   I said *no,* and I mean *no."* Mom pulls me by my arm out the door and through the parking lot.

I think about my wish. I guess mall fountains don't work nearly as well as wish ponds. As we head toward our car, I look over my shoulder at the Mall Madness sign.

I have mall madness. But it's definitely not the excited kind.

A PARENT CONFERENCE

"For you." I walk into the kitchen and hand my parents an envelope.

Mom puts the envelope down on the counter and hands me the phone.

Most days, I love phone calls. But not today. Today, I have something important that I need to do. "Hello," I say in my *I'm-not-in-the-mood-to-talk* voice.

"Hey!" says Joey. "Want to meet by the wish pond in five minutes? If you bring Cheeseburger, I can try to teach her to dance on her back legs. I saw someone teaching a cat to dance on TV and I . . . "

But I don't let Joey finish. "Maybe later," I tell him. Right now, I don't have time to teach my cat to dance.

I pick up the envelope off of the counter. "You need to open this," I say to Mom.

Mom smiles as she takes it from me, but she stops smiling when she sees what's written on the outside. "A Parent Conference," she says out loud.

"I wonder why Mrs. Daily wants to see us?" Dad says.

Mom opens the envelope, and when she reads the note inside, she starts smiling again. "Mrs. Daily doesn't want to see us," Mom says. "Mallory does."

"It's conference time," I tell my parents. I pull two chairs together so my parents can sit down. I talk to them like I'm a teacher. "We need to talk about Mallory."

"Is she OK?" asks Dad. He looks like he's trying not to laugh.

I give Dad a *this-is-serious* look. "Mallory is OK, but she could be doing better."

"Really?" asks Mom. "How could she be doing better?"

I give my parents an encouraging look.

"I wasn't going to tell you this, but since you asked . . ." I stop talking. I feel like I've got an extra-large peanut butter and marshmallow sandwich stuck in my throat.

Telling parents how their child could be doing better isn't as easy as I thought. Especially if you're about to tell them something they might not want to hear.

Dad looks at his watch. "Sweet Potato, I

have to get to work. The store opens early on Saturdays. Can you tell us quickly what the problem is?"

I clear my throat. "It's complicated."

"Let's un-complicate it," he says. "I'll start a sentence, and you fill in the blank."

I nod my head. "OK."

"Here goes," says Dad. "I invited my parents to a conference to tell them I could be doing better if . . . Now, you fill in the rest of the sentence."

Even though it's not easy, I finish Dad's sentence.

"I invited my parents to a conference to tell them I could be doing better if they would buy me the Perfect Purse."

"Mallory, we've discussed this!" says Mom. "That purse is expensive and unnecessary. I can't think of one good reason to buy it."

"I can," I tell Mom. "I can think of ten *very* good reasons to buy the Perfect Purse."

Before Mom or Dad can say anything else, I start reading.

10 Reasons Why I, Mallory McDonald, <u>Need</u> to Buy the Perfect Purse:

#<u>1</u>: The Perfect Purse is stylish. It comes with 10 designer covers.

#<u>2</u>: The Perfect Purse is special. It comes with a sparkly pin.

#<u>3</u>: The Perfect Purse is versatile. You can use it as a purse, a tote, or a carryall.

#<u>4</u>: The Perfect Purse is practical. It has a waterproof cover for rainy days.

#5: The Perfect Purse is economical. You will never have to buy another purse.

#6: The Perfect Purse is exclusive. Limited quantities are available.

#7: The Perfect Purse is chic. Fashionable girls everywhere are carrying it.

#8: I will love having the Perfect Purse. It will be like having a new best friend.

#9: Mary Ann is getting the Perfect Purse. I need to get one so we can match.

#10: If I get the Perfect Purse, I will be perfectly happy. My happiness will make me a better daughter, a better sister, and a better student too.

"Mallory, you sound like a commercial," Dad says when I finish reading.

"Even worse than sounding like a commercial," says Mom, "is that you sound spoiled. Just because Mary Ann is getting one, doesn't mean that you can too."

"But I *need* to get one. Mary Ann and I are planning to get matching purses. Please," I say to my parents.

"You and Mary Ann don't always get the same things," Mom says. "She didn't get a cat when you got Cheeseburger."

I don't know how we got on the subject of cats when we are supposed to be talking about purses. "I didn't get a cat," I remind Mom. "I found her."

"Everyone gets different things," says Dad. "And you're not getting the purse."

"Will you at least think about it?" I ask.

But both of my parents shake their

heads *no* at the same time. "Mallory, this is the last time we're going to discuss this," says Mom.

Mom stands up. "Conference time is over." She puts her chair back at the table.

Dad puts his chair back too. He kisses me on the forehead. "I'm going to work."

After Dad leaves, I go into the family room and plop down on the couch with Cheeseburger. Max and his dog, Champ, are watching a show I don't even like. But I

don't care.   All I can think about is my
parent conference.

My conference didn't go well. If parents
got graded on conference behavior, my
parents would get a "U" for uncooperative.

When I hear the mail truck, I run
outside to see if I got anything. The
postman hands me a stack of letters. Joey
is playing in his front yard. He
waves to me.

I wave back, then
I look through the
mail to see if
there's anything
for me, and there
is . . . a letter from
Mary Ann! I sit
down in front of
the mailbox and
rip it open.

Dear Mallory,

Good news! My mom bought me the Perfect Purse!

I can't wait till I wear mine!

I can't wait till you wear yours!

I can't wait till we match! See you soon, and when I do, everything will be perfect, perfect, perfect . . . especially our purses!

Love,

Mary Ann

When I'm done reading, I lean back against the mailbox. I can feel the cold steel of the pole through my sweater. Mary Ann is wrong about one thing. Everything will not be perfect, perfect, perfect . . . not if I don't have the Perfect Purse too.

While I'm busy imagining Mary Ann with

her purse, and me without mine, Joey walks
over to our front porch. "Want me to
teach Cheeseburger some tricks now?"

I shake my head *no*.

"Feel like skateboarding?"

I shake my head *no* again.

"We could just go down to the wish pond
and skip rocks."

I shake my head *no* a third time. "I don't
feel like it."

Joey makes a mad face. "You never feel like playing anymore."

"I'm sorry," I tell Joey. I don't want him to think I don't want to be his friend.

I try to explain about the Perfect Purse.

When I'm done explaining, I look at Joey. He always understands things. But this time, he doesn't look like he understands at all.

"Mallory, who cares about a dumb old purse?"

Even though I can see Joey doesn't care, I do, and I know someone else who might care too. "We can play some other time," I tell Joey.

I scoop up Cheeseburger. "Right now, I have to make a phone call."

A PHONE CALL

I tiptoe up the stairs into Mom and Dad's room. I put Cheeseburger down on a chair and close the door. I pick up the receiver and punch the buttons on the keypad.

When the phone starts ringing, I cross my toes. I hope the person I'm calling is home because I really need to talk to her.

The phone rings. Once. Twice. Three times. Finally a voice answers.

"Hello."

"Grandma!" I scream. "Surprise! It's me, Mallory!"

"What a wonderful surprise!" says Grandma. "How's my little Honey Bee?"

"Not so good," I tell her.

"Oh no!" says Grandma like she can't think of anything worse than me not feeling good. "Do you want to tell me what's the matter? Maybe I can help."

"I hope you can help me, because Mom and Dad haven't been any help at all."

"I'm all ears," says Grandma.

I giggle. I know Grandma means she's listening to every word I'm saying, but I can't help imagining what Grandma would look like if she were all ears.

"Here's the problem. There's this purse called the Perfect Purse . . ." And before I can stop myself, I start telling Grandma everything about the Perfect Purse.

"It's the latest and the greatest and it comes with ten covers and a sparkly pin and Mary Ann is getting one and I want one so we can match and . . ."

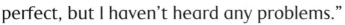

"Whoa!" Grandma laughs. "Slow down. So far I've heard lots of reasons why the purse is perfect, but I haven't heard any problems."

"There is a problem," I tell Grandma in my *there's-only-one-problem-but-it's-a-big-one* voice. "Mom and Dad won't get it for me.

"And that's where I come in?" asks Grandma.

"Exactly!" I say.

"Well," says Grandma. "You've come to the right person. I think I can help you."

I knew Grandma would understand. "So you'll get the Perfect Purse for me?"

Grandma laughs again. "Honey Bee, I'm going to help you get the Perfect Purse."

"What do you mean?" I ask, even though I'm not sure I really want to know.

Grandma sighs into the phone. "Mallory, I'm going to tell you a story."

I sit back on the bed. Now I think it's my turn to be all ears.

"When I was a young girl, there was a doll I wanted," says Grandma. "She had glass eyes and real hair and her clothes were made of the finest silk. One day I tore a picture of the doll out of a magazine and showed it to my parents."

"Did they get it for you?" I ask.

"No, they didn't get it for me, even though I begged and pleaded and promised I would do anything if they would just get me the doll."

Grandma's parents sound a lot like mine.

Grandma continues her story. "My parents told me the doll was very expensive, and that even though she was beautiful, they thought she was a silly waste of money."

"So what did you do?"

"I decided to buy the doll myself."

Grandma must have gotten a lot of birthday money that year. "So you had enough to pay for the doll yourself?"

"Not exactly. I had to go to work to make enough money to buy the doll."

"But you were just a kid," I remind Grandma. "Wasn't

it hard to make money?"

"It was indeed," says Grandma. "But I started a business going door to door selling oranges for a penny until I had enough to buy the doll."

I think about how much the Perfect Purse costs. "I think I'll have to sell a lot of oranges to buy what I want."

"Maybe you want to do something other than sell oranges."

"Like what?" I ask Grandma.

"Give it some thought," says Grandma. "Talk to some people. I'm sure you'll come up with something."

The only thing I wanted to be thinking about after this phone call was carrying a purse, not starting a business.

"Good luck, Honey Bee, and let me know what happens." Grandma blows me kisses over the phone before she hangs up.

I pick up Cheeseburger and walk back downstairs to my room. Maybe Grandma is right. Maybe that is what I need to do.

Once, I saw a TV interview of Fashion Fran. She started her first business selling hand-painted T-shirts. She said she couldn't believe how many people bought her T-shirts. Maybe I should sell something too.

I take Cheeseburger into my closet to look for things to sell. I see lots of things, but no things I want to sell.

I sit down at my desk and take out a sheet of paper. I write *Things I Can Sell* on the top of the paper. I try to write a list of things I can sell, but the only thing I can think about is writing a letter.

I take out a fresh sheet of paper and begin.

Dear Mary Ann,

This is a letter, but it's not a regular letter. It's a business letter.

(A business letter is a letter you write when you're going into business, and that's exactly what I'm planning to do.)

I bet you have a lot of questions like: Why am I going into business and what

kind of business am I going into? Well,
here are some answers.

I am going into business because I have
to ... if I want to get the Perfect Purse.

And I don't have any idea what kind of
business I'm going into. But I do know
this: I'm going to
sell something
that a lot
of people
will want to
buy so I can
get the Perfect Purse and
we can match when you come to visit.

I think that sounds like a good plan,
don't you?

Well, that's all for now. I've got to go
start my business. You will be here soon,
soon, soon. And when you get here, I
want to make sure I have the Perfect

Purse too.

(So don't worry, by the time you get here, we will match, match, match.)

Yours truly (I think that's how you end a business letter),

Mallory

When I'm done writing, I stick my business letter in an envelope. Now all I have to do is go start a business. How hard can it be?

WHAT A JOKE!

When I walk into the kitchen, Mom and Max are sitting at the table. Mom smiles at me. "Max and I are putting together a list of who he wants to invite to his birthday dinner."

"Yeah," says Max, "so make like a tree and leave."

Mom gives Max an *if-you-can't-say-something-nice-don't-say-anything* look.

I almost forgot my brother is turning

eleven in two weeks. I hope when he does, he starts acting his age. "I don't want to interrupt, but I need a box."

"Are you moving?" asks Max. "If you are, I'll help you pack."

I ignore Max. I know he isn't really trying to be helpful. "I'm not moving. I'm starting a business selling joke books. I need a box for my books," I tell Mom.

Max laughs. "You're starting a joke book selling business?" Max laughs even harder. "What a joke!"

Mom puts down her pencil. "Honey, why would you sell your joke books?"

I love my joke books. Grandma gave me my first one when I learned to read. I've been collecting them ever since.

But here's the thing: I think other people will love them too.

"I'm selling them because I need

money," I tell Mom.

Mom frowns. "Mallory, what do you need money for?"

I scratch my head and do some fast thinking. I know Mom won't like hearing that I need money to buy the Perfect Purse, but there's something else I think Mom *will* like hearing. I look at Max. "I need money to buy Max's birthday present."

The frown on Mom's face turns into a smile. "That is very sweet," she says. "But you don't have to sell your joke books to buy a present for your brother."

I look at Max. "I want to."

Max smiles like he likes the idea that I'm willing to sell my joke books to buy him a birthday present, but that he can't believe that I am.

I smile back. With *part* of the money, I am going to buy him a present. And with the other part, I'm going to buy what I want.

I pull a square of paper out of my pocket and hand it to Mom. "Here's my card."

Mom reads from the card. "Joke books for sale. Contact Mallory McDonald at 17 Wish Pond Road. Ha ha! Tee hee!" Mom smiles, then she gets a serious look on her face. "Mallory, who are you planning to sell your joke books to?"

I knew Mom would ask me that question, and I've already thought of an answer.

"I'm going to go next door to the Winstons'. I'll ask Mrs. Black down the street. I'll ask the other neighbors. I'll call Pamela. And I'll ask my other friends at school. I'll sell a joke book to anybody that wants to buy one."

Mom puts her arm around me. "It's hard work finding something that people want to buy."

"Good luck," says Max. But I can tell by looking at him that he's not so sure my plan is going to work. But I think it's going to.

I think of Grandma and her oranges. I'd rather buy a joke book than a piece of fruit. "All I can do is try," I tell Mom.

Mom pats me on the head. "There's a box in the laundry room you can use."

I get the box and take it into my room. I fill it with joke books and write *Joke Books* on the side of the box.

Then I walk down to the wish pond with my box and make a wish. *I wish I sell a lot of joke books.* Mary Ann will be here next weekend, and I want to have my purse when she gets here.

I walk to the Winstons' and ring the bell. When Winnie answers the door, she looks at my box. "What do you want?" she asks.

I feel like a Girl Scout selling cookies. "Want to buy a joke book?"

Winnie snorts. "Get a life. I'll go get Joey."

I wish joke books came in yummy flavors like thin mint or peanut butter sandwich. If they did, they'd be easier to sell.

When Joey comes to the door, I explain what I'm selling.

Joey looks through my box. "I love joke books. But I'm saving my money to buy a new skateboard."

He points down the street. "Why don't you try Mrs. Black. She buys everything."

I walk to Mrs. Black's house and ring the doorbell. "I'm selling joke books," I tell her

when she opens the door. "Would you like to buy one?"

Mrs. Black frowns. "I like candy, cookies, and wrapping paper. But I'm afraid I'm the wrong person for a joke book. Perhaps you'll have better luck at another house."

But I don't have luck at any other houses, even though I go to every single one of them on my street. No one wants to buy a joke book.

I walk home with my box. Even though I didn't add any books to it, it feels heavier than it did before.

When I get home, I go into the kitchen and call Pamela. I hope she will be my first customer.

"Hi Pamela, want to buy a joke book?" I ask in my cheeriest voice when she answers. I tell her all about the different joke books I'm selling.

"Hold on," says Pamela. "Let me ask my mom."

I cross my toes while I wait. I hope Pamela's mom says yes.

But she doesn't. "Sorry," says Pamela. "I can't buy a joke book."

"That's OK," I mumble into the phone. I tell Pamela good-bye and carry my box of books to my room and drop it on the floor. I sit down on the box and pull Cheeseburger into my lap. "No one wanted to buy a joke book," I tell her.

Max sticks his head into my room. "No luck, huh?"

I can't believe Max was listening to my private conversation with my cat. I'm sure he's going to remind me that selling joke books was a big joke.

"OUT!" I say to my brother.

But Max doesn't go out. He comes into

my room and sits down on my floor.

"I'm just trying to help," he says. "Think about it from my perspective. If you don't sell something soon, I'm not getting much of a birthday present. Let me give you a little advice," says Max. "If at first you don't succeed, try again."

"Thanks a lot," I mumble. The only thing I'd like to succeed at is selling my brother.

A BUSINESS
FLOP

Dear Mary Ann,

I am a business flop.
If you don't know what that means, I'll tell you.
It means I stink at business! That's right. I tried four businesses in four days

and each one was a big, fat failure. Keep
reading and you will see what I mean.

BUSINESS FLOP #1:
JOKE BOOK SELLING BUSINESS
　　I tried selling my joke books.
　　I tried to sell them to my friends. I
tried to sell them to my neighbors. I tried
to sell them to anyone that I thought
might buy one. And guess what . . . NO
ONE did.
　　I didn't sell one joke book.
　　This business was a big flop.

BUSINESS FLOP #2:
GIRL FOR HIRE
　　I tried to work for people.
　　I told people that I would do anything
they wanted me to do, and all they had
to do was pay me. At first, this seemed

like a good idea.

I worked for Mom. I made her lunch. She paid me a quarter.

I worked for Dad. I swept the garage. He paid me fifty cents.

I worked for Max. I cleaned his room. He paid me a dime.

I worked for Joey. I put his socks into pairs. He paid me a nickel.

I worked for Winnie. I folded her clothes. She paid me another nickel.

I worked all day and all I made was ninety-five cents!

That is not a lot of money to make for a hard day's work.

This business was an even bigger flop.

BUSINESS FLOP #3:
SKATEBOARDING DEMONSTRATIONS

I thought this was my best business idea ever. I wanted Joey to do skateboarding demonstrations. People would pay to see him and he would pay me for coming up with this great idea.

Here's the good news:

Joey wanted to do it and people wanted to pay to see him do it.

Here's the bad news:

Joey didn't want to pay me for coming up with the idea. He said he'd been thinking about doing skateboarding demonstrations for a long time, and that even though I'm his good friend, he didn't know why he should pay me if he had to do all the work.

Are you starting to see what I mean about me being a business flop?

BUSINESS FLOP #4:
COMIC STRIP STAND

You're probably thinking it is impossible for another business to flop, but trust me, this business was the biggest flop of all.

I decided to sell cartoons. I set up a stand in the front yard. I got out all my paper and pencils. I was ready to draw.

But nobody came to get a comic. Nobody.

Well, actually Mom came. I drew one comic strip for her (see end of this letter), but she said she wouldn't buy it because it was too negative. So I didn't sell any comic strips.

See, I told you: I AM A BIG, FAT BUSINESS FLOP. And if you ask me, being a business flop is almost as bad as doing a bellyflop.

Now I can't buy the Perfect Purse, so we can't have matching purses.

I thought I would have fun being in business. I thought I would make a lot of money. I thought I would be able to buy whatever I wanted. But I think when it comes to business, all I have are dumb ideas.

I wish there was some kind of business where I could have fun and make a lot of money. Like a salon. Wouldn't that be fun? We could do it together.

We could do hair and nails and makeup. We could give out little cookies with M's on top. And we could wear matching T-shirts.

Maybe that's what we'll do when we grow up. Maybe then I can buy the Perfect Purse. (Do you think they will run out of them before we are grown-ups?)

I hope this letter did not make you too sad.

It makes me sad.

My tears are about to fall out on this page,

Mallory

P.S. Here is the comic strip I drew for Mom. (And don't worry, you don't have to pay me for it.)

TALE OF A BUSINESS FLOP
written and illustrated by Mallory McDonald

MARY ANN TO THE RESCUE

Dear Mallory,

I got your letter.

I'm sorry to hear you think you're a business flop (at least you're not a flip-flop).

You might think your ideas are dumb, but I don't.

I love, love, love your salon idea!!!!!!!!!!!!!!!!!!!

It would be so much fun to have our own salon.

Everything would be just like you said it would be.

Hey, maybe we don't have to wait until we grow up. (Don't forget, we won't be grown-ups for a long time.) Maybe we can have a salon now. (Not right now, but this weekend when I come to visit.)

Wouldn't that be fun, fun, fun?!?

What do you think?

See you in a few days.

Can't wait, wait, wait!

Hugs and kisses,
Mary Ann

I fold Mary Ann's letter and put it on my desk.

"Maybe Mary Ann is right," I say to Cheeseburger.

Maybe we don't have to wait until we're grown-ups to have a salon. Maybe Mary Ann and I *can* have a salon when she comes to town this weekend with her mom.

The more I think about it, the more I love, love, love the idea.

SALON MALLORY

Ding-dong.

"I'll get it!" Mary Ann and I yell at the same time. We run down the hall to open the front door. But before we do, we do one final check.

T-shirts. Check. We're wearing the matching *Salon Mallory* T-shirts we made.

Hair. Check. We pinned up our hair with

coordinating hair clips.

Nails. Check. We painted our fingernails ten different colors.

Since the moment Mary Ann arrived in Fern Falls, we've been working hard to

make sure *Salon Mallory* is a big success.

Last night, we called my friends in my class to remind them about their salon appointments. We set up hair, nail, and makeup stations in my room. We even made a big sign that says *Salon Mallory* to hang on the door of my room.

This morning, we're ready for business. Mary Ann and I look at each other and nod. "Welcome to *Salon Mallory!*" we say as we fling the front door open.

Pamela, April, Danielle, Arielle, Brittany, Dawn, Emma, and Grace are there, and so is Jackson.

Mary Ann giggles. "We didn't expect any boys," she whispers to me.

"Jackson, what are you doing here?" I ask.

He takes a notebook and pencil out of his pocket. "When Mrs. Daily heard about the salon, she said I should come write an article about it for *The Daily News.*"

"Wow!" says Mary Ann. "We're going to be famous!"

"*The Daily News* is the school newspaper that our classroom writes," I explain to my best friend.

"Who cares which newspaper we're going to be in," shrieks Mary Ann. "We're going to be in a newspaper! Follow me," she says to all my friends.

Everyone walks down the hall behind Mary Ann.

As we walk toward my room, I make a wish in my head. *I wish this business won't flop like my other businesses.*

When we get to my room, I start on hair, and Mary Ann does makeup.

"Over here." I point Pamela to the hair station. I brush and braid her hair.

"Can you tie a ribbon in it?" asks Pamela.

I give Pamela a big box of ribbons to choose from. She picks a yellow one, and I tie it onto the bottom of her braid.

Mary Ann leads Danielle and Arielle over to the makeup table. "You can pick whatever color eye shadow you like."

"I want violet." Danielle points to a shimmery, light purple.

"Me too," says Arielle.

Mary Ann dabs matching shadow on both of their lids.

While I'm combing out Brittany's hair, and Mary Ann is brushing lip gloss on Emma, Max sticks his head in my room. "What's going on in here?" he asks.

Mary Ann stops brushing. "We're trying to earn money so Mallory can buy . . ."

But I cough before Mary Ann can say *the Perfect Purse.* And I keep coughing. Max doesn't need to know that I'm planning to buy a present AND a purse.

Mary Ann goes back to brushing lip gloss on Emma. "I don't see your name on the appointment book," she says to Max. "No need to stick around, unless you want your hair or makeup done."

Usually, Max would say something

obnoxious to Mary Ann, but he surprises me. He just gives me an *I-think-salons-are-stupid-but-if-that's-what-you-have-to-do-to-buy-me-a-birthday-present-then-it's-okay-with-me* look.

Max walks out. I go back to combing and braiding. Mary Ann keeps brushing

and dabbing. We don't stop all morning.

Jackson sits at my desk taking notes. Then he takes out a camera. "I need a picture to go with the article." He takes a few shots while we work.

"Wow!" says Emma when she sees her makeup. "I look like I'm eleven." Everyone looks in my mirror . . . and everyone looks like they're happy.

When we finish with hair and makeup, Mary Ann and I start on nails.

"We have ten different colors of polishes, and you can choose whatever combination you like," I tell my friends.

Our customers start looking through the bottles of polish at the nail station.

"I want light yellow," Pamela says.

April wants green with blue dots.

Danielle and Arielle choose purple to match their eye shadow.

Brittany, Dawn, Emma, and Grace want the same thing Mary Ann and I have . . . ten fingers, ten colors.

While everyone is letting their nails dry, Mom comes into my room with the platter of cookies with M's on top and the lemonade Mary Ann and I made last night.

"Those cookies are so cute!" says Grace.

Mom puts the platter down. She smiles like she approves of the results at *Salon Mallory.* "Be careful," says Mom. "You don't want to mess up your nails."

Everyone eats cookies and drinks lemonade like they're fancy ladies at a tea party. When they're through, they pay us and get ready to leave.

"Thanks for coming to *Salon Mallory!*" Mary Ann and I wave good-bye.

"Phew!" Mary Ann collapses on my bed after everyone is gone. "That was a lot of work." She takes a deep breath like all that brushing and painting made her tired.

I'm tired too, but not too tired to count what we earned this morning. I start to make neat stacks of all the coins, but Mary Ann pushes them into one big pile. "You don't need to count it," she says. "Just look how much is there."

I eye the money on my floor. Mary Ann

is right. There is a lot. "I'm going to have to wear pants with big pockets to take all that to the mall tomorrow," I say.

Mary Ann giggles. We start pushing money through the little slot on the tip of my piggy bank. While we're pushing, Joey knocks on my window. I get up and open it. "Want to come outside and play?" he asks Mary Ann and me.

"Maybe later," says Mary Ann before I even have time to answer.

Joey nods at Mary Ann like it's no problem, but then he looks at me like it is a problem. I can tell Joey is upset.

I start to say *sorry,* but before I do, Joey walks away.

I feel like ever since Mary Ann and I agreed to get matching Perfect Purses, I've been so busy trying to think of how I'm going to get mine, I haven't had time to play with Joey. The problem is, I don't know what to do about it.

If I ever get the Perfect Purse, I'll be glad to have it for two reasons.

One: I can't wait to have it.

Two: I can't wait to be done getting it.

After Joey leaves, Mary Ann and I go back to pushing coins into my piggy bank. When we're done, I pick it up and shake it. It's so full, it barely makes a noise when I shake it. It's heavy too.

I hand it to Mary Ann so she can feel it. "I can't believe how much you have," she says.

"I probably have enough to buy ten Perfect Purses and a birthday present for Max," I tell her. "And I couldn't have done it without you."

"That's what best friends are for." Mary Ann hands me her Perfect Purse. "Here, try this on."

I hold her purse and model it in front of the mirror. "How do I look?"

"Cute, cute, cute!" squeals Mary Ann. "I can't wait to go to the mall tomorrow! We're going to have matching purses! We can wear them to dinner tomorrow night."

Mary Ann jumps around and hugs me. Even though my best friend gets excited about a lot of things, I haven't seen her this excited in a long time.

Seeing her excited makes me excited too. It will be fun having matching purses. I hug Mary Ann back, and then I pick up Cheeseburger and hug her too. I know tomorrow will be the best, best, best day ever.

I can't think of anything that could mess it up.

DECISIONS, DECISIONS

"Mallory, hurry up. You came to the mall to buy a birthday present for your brother." Mom taps her foot like she's getting impatient with me.

I know one of the things I planned to buy was a present for Max. But when I made that plan, I didn't know I'd barely have enough money to buy what I wanted for myself.

Mom was right about one thing . . . the only NOT perfect thing about the Perfect Purse is the price. I can't believe how much it costs!

There's no way I can buy the purse *and* a present. I put the Perfect Purse that I'm holding back on the display.

"C'mon!" Mary Ann picks up the purse and pulls on my sleeve. "We came to get the Perfect Purse, so get it."

Mom puts her hand on my back and pushes me away from the purse display. "Why don't we go look in Sporting Goods? Max might like some baseball cards."

Mary Ann keeps pulling. Mom keeps pushing. I feel like Mom and Mary Ann are playing tug-of-war and the rope that they're pulling on is me.

I don't think Mom understands that

buying a present for Max isn't so simple. I know Max will be a little upset if I don't get him a birthday present, but Mary Ann will be a LOT upset if I don't get the purse.

I wish I didn't have to choose, but that's a wish I know won't come true.

I try to explain things to Mom. "Mary Ann and I worked hard yesterday to make enough money so we can have matching purses. I only have enough to buy the Perfect Purse. I don't have enough to buy the purse *and* a present for Max."

I think I explained things pretty well.

I cross my toes. I hope Mom understands. But she doesn't look like she does. Mom crosses something too, and it's not her toes.

She crosses her arms across her chest. "Mallory, I understand that you want to buy the purse. And I understand that Mary

Ann wants you to have it. But it's your brother's birthday. Don't you think you should get him something?"

"She could make him a card," says Mary Ann.

Sometimes my best friend has the best ideas, and this is one of those times.

"That's a great idea!" I say to Mom. "You know I'm good at making things. I'll make Max a really special card."

But I can tell by the look on Mom's face that she doesn't think making Max a card is nearly as good an idea as Mary Ann and I think it is.

Mom puts her hand on my arm. "Mary Ann, will you excuse us for a minute? Mallory and I need to have a word alone." Mom pulls me over to the other side of the purse display and starts whispering.

"Mallory, you have a decision to make.

90

You can either buy the Perfect Purse with all of your money or you can buy your brother a birthday present with some of it and have some left over to buy something for yourself."

I start to say something, but Mom holds her finger up, which I know means she's not done talking yet.

"I'm sure you know how I feel about this. We've already talked about the price of the Perfect Purse. There are lots of other, less expensive purses. You're nine years old, and I'm going to let you make your own decision."

Then Mom looks at me in a very serious way. "I'm counting on you to make the right decision." I follow Mom as she walks back toward Mary Ann.

On the one hand, I really want the Perfect Purse. I worked hard to get it, and so did Mary Ann. I know she will be disappointed if I don't get it.

On the other hand, I know if I don't get Max a birthday present, Mom will be unhappy with me. Max will be disappointed too.

I know I have to make a decision. The problem is . . . it's a hard decision to make. I look at Mom. She looks like she's waiting for me to make one decision. I look at Mary Ann. She looks like she's waiting for me to make another decision.

I think about doing eenie, meenie, miney, mo to help me decide, but I don't think that's the answer.

"C'mon!" Mary Ann tugs on me. "What are you waiting for?"

I try to explain, but the words won't come out of my mouth.

Mary Ann puts her arm around me and

looks at Mom. "Will you excuse us for a minute?" she says. "Mallory and I need to have a word alone."

Mary Ann steers me away from Mom and starts whispering. "Earth to Mallory," she says in a low voice. "You're talking about Max. Max who is mean to you. Max who is mean to me. Max who doesn't even let you watch your favorite TV show."

Maybe Mary Ann is right. Max can be mean, and he does change the channel whenever *Fashion Fran* is on. "But he is my brother and it is his birthday and he did get me something on my birthday," I tell Mary Ann.

"And you're going to make him a very special card," says Mary Ann.

She steers me back over to the purse display. She picks up a purse and lays it gently in my arms. "C'mon, Mal."

I look down at the Perfect Purse . . . the shiny, beautiful Perfect Purse. Lying there in my arms, it really does look perfect.

Mary Ann is right. I will make Max a card. I will make him a very special card with my best paper and glitter and stickers.

I look up at Mary Ann and even though the corner of my lip barely curls upwards, she knows me well enough to know what

I'm thinking.

Mary Ann throws her arms around me. "We're going to have so much fun having matching purses, and we can start wearing them tonight! You made the right decision," she says smiling.

I sure hope Mary Ann is right. I smile back at her, but I'm scared to even look at Mom. Something tells me she's not smiling.

A BAD NIGHT

"Good night," says Mary Ann. "Sleep tight and don't let the bedbugs bite."

"Good night." I tell Mary Ann to sleep tight and not to let the bedbugs bite too. I hope they don't bite my best friend, but right now, I don't care if they chew me to bits.

Even though Mary Ann and I told each other good night, I think tonight was a bad night. If I had a diary, which I don't, this is what I'd write in it.

96

Dear Diary,

Tonight I went to the Fondue Pot with my family, the Winstons, and Mary Ann and her mom.

Most Saturday nights, the grown-ups go out and the kids stay home. But tonight, the grown-ups took the kids out to dinner with them.

Mom said it was going to be a special night. But if you ask me, it was an especially bad night.

It didn't start out that way. It started out especially good.

First, Mary Ann and I got dressed alike. We wore matching shirts, skirts, and shoes. And matching purses . . . matching Perfect Purses with polka dot covers. Everybody said we looked cute, cute, cute.

That was the good part of the night. Here's where it all went wrong.

When we got to the restaurant, the waitress brought two fondue pots to the table. One was full of melted cheese and the other one was filled with hot oil.

She gave us these long forks called fondue forks and told us to use them for dipping and cooking.

We dipped pieces of bread in the melted cheese pot. Then we cooked little chunks of chicken and steak in the pot full of hot oil.

I know, you're thinking all that sounds good, and it was. But I haven't gotten to the bad part yet. Here's the bad part.

After dinner, we had chocolate fondue for dessert. The waitress brought a big pot full of melted chocolate to the table. Then she put down a tray of graham crackers, marshmallows, strawberries, and angel food cake. She said we could dip everything in the chocolate for dessert.

I bet you're thinking this sounds like the best part of all, but here's why it wasn't.

Joey stuck his fondue fork in a marshmallow. Then he stuck the marshmallow in the chocolate. When it was all covered in chocolate, he pulled it out. The chocolate covered marshmallow was supposed to go into his mouth, but it didn't.

It fell off his fork and it landed on my Perfect Purse!

Mr. Winston and Mary Ann's mom tried to clean off my purse with their

napkins, but it only made it look worse. Joey said he was sorry, that it was an accident.

Then everybody had something to say:

"You shouldn't have put your purse on the table," said Winnie.

"Who cares about a stupid purse anyway?" said Max.

"The chocolate spot looks like a polka dot," said Dad.

"We can try to wash it when we get home," said Mom.

"You still have nine other covers," said Mary Ann.

She put her arm around me and smiled. But I could tell she was glad Joey didn't spill melted chocolate on her purse.

Everybody kept eating chocolate

fondue, but I felt so awful, I couldn't even enjoy what I know would have been my favorite dessert ever.

In the van on the way home, Mary Ann said she could tell that I was really upset about what happened in the restaurant. Then she said that she is so, so, so glad we got matching Perfect Purses, even if one of my covers has a chocolate stain on it.

She asked me if I was still glad too.

I told her I was. But here's something I didn't tell Mary Ann.

I'm not sure if I am.

So far, owning the Perfect Purse hasn't been as perfect as I thought it would be.

I know Mary Ann loves having hers. I know I really wanted to get mine. But I'm not having as much fun having it as I thought I would. All you can do is put stuff in it and take it places, and then it just gets dirty.

The end.

Mallory

I pull Cheeseburger close to me, then I close two things: my pretend journal and my eyes.

THE WORST DAY

Usually, I hate getting up for school, but not today.

Today, I pop out of bed and pull on my stretchy velvet pants and striped turtleneck. Then, I snap my leopard print purse cover onto my Perfect Purse. I can't wait to go to school because I'm taking my Perfect Purse with me.

Even though I didn't have fun using my Perfect Purse at dinner, I went to a lot of trouble to get it, so today I'm giving it a second chance.

Today is going to be the best day ever!

When I'm finished snapping, I hold my purse in my hand and look in the mirror. "You look *mah-va-lous dahl-ing,*" I say to myself. Actually, I think I look like a movie star. I give Cheeseburger a movie star kiss on each cheek, and then I head down the hall.

"Mallory, we're having eggs," Mom says when I walk into the kitchen.

I peek in the pan. The eggs look squishy and jiggly. I bet movie stars don't eat squishy, jiggly eggs for breakfast.

"I'll just have a granola bar," I tell Mom. I take one from the box in the pantry.

Mom plucks the granola bar out of my hand and puts the plate of eggs in front of me. "Just a few bites," she says.

Even though eating eggs is the last thing I want to do this morning, I take a few bites. Nothing is going to mess up my day today, not even squishy eggs.

When I'm done, I kiss Mom on the cheek. "Got to run," I tell her.

"What's the rush?" she asks.

"I just can't wait to get to school," I tell Mom.

She rumples my hair. "I like seeing you so enthusiastic."

I am enthusiastic. I can't wait to show my Perfect Purse to my friends. I can already hear what they're going to say:

"*That purse is so cool!*" Pamela will say.

"*That purse is so awesome!*" Arielle will say.

"What a lovely purse!" Mrs. Daily will say with a big smile.

I stop next door at the Winston's to get Joey. "Notice anything different?" I ask as we walk to school.

Joey looks at me. "You look the same to me as you always look."

Joey must need to have his eyes tested. "Look again," I tell him.

Joey looks up at my head, then down at my feet. "Nothing," he says.

Joey looked at the top and at the bottom. But I don't think he did a good job looking at the middle. I move my Perfect Purse so I'm holding it right in front of my body . . . right where Joey can see it. "Now do you see anything different?" I ask.

Joey shakes his head. "Move the purse and maybe I can tell."

Even though Joey is one of my best

friends, sometimes he acts like such a boy.
I wave my purse in front of his face. "This is
what's different," I tell him. "What do you
think of this cover?"

Joey groans. "Enough with this purse
stuff. That's all you ever talk about
anymore." Joey walks ahead of me until he
gets to Room 310.

When I walk into the classroom, Mrs.
Daily tells everyone to take their seats.

"Let's get started," she says. "Please take out your math books."

I take out my math book and so does my desk mate, Pamela.

"Please turn to page 112," says Mrs. Daily.

Pamela starts turning pages in her book, but I stop her. I lay my Perfect Purse down on top of her math book. "Look!" I whisper to Pamela. "What do you think?"

I wait for Pamela to tell me she thinks my purse is cool, but that's not what she tells me. "Mallory, put that away." Pamela tries to scoot the purse off her side of the desk. "We're going to get in trouble," she whispers.

"Girls," Mrs. Daily looks in our direction, "are you paying attention?"

Pamela looks toward the front of the room at Mrs. Daily's desk and nods like the answer is *yes, we are paying attention.*

Maybe she is, but I don't know how anyone could pay attention to math when there are much more exciting things to pay attention to . . . like a new purse.

I turn around in my seat to Danielle and Arielle's desks. "Look!" I say in my *you-won't-believe-what-I-have* voice. I wave my Perfect Purse in front of their faces. "Do you like my purse?" I wait for them to say it is so *awesome*.

But they don't. Arielle blows out her breath. "That purse is so last year," she whispers.

What? I can't believe what I just heard! Arielle is wrong, wrong, wrong! "This purse is so *not* last year," I start to explain to her.

"Girls! What's going on back there?" Mrs. Daily asks from the front of the classroom.

"Nothing," says Arielle out loud.

"We're in the middle of math," Danielle whispers to me like I'm preventing her from learning something that she really cares about.

But I know Danielle doesn't care all that much about math. "Did you know this purse comes with ten designer covers?" I whisper to her.

I start to tell her about the sparkly butterfly pin, but before I do, someone says my name.

"Mallory!"

I turn around slowly. Mrs. Daily is standing in front of my desk. "What is going on back here?"

"We're trying to pay attention," says Arielle, "but Mallory keeps trying to show us her new purse."

Mrs. Daily looks down at the purse in my hands. I can tell by the way she's looking at it that she doesn't think it is lovely like I thought she would.

Suddenly, my Perfect Purse doesn't feel so perfect.

"Mallory, why don't you give me the purse, and I'll keep it on my desk." She reaches out her hand to take it from me.

I feel like Dorothy in *The Wizard of Oz* when the Wicked Witch tries to take her ruby slippers.

I clutch my purse to me to keep it safe, but Mrs. Daily pulls it out of my hands. "I'll keep it until the end of the day. You can have it when school is over," she says.

I look down at my empty hands.

When I woke up this morning, I thought today would be the best day ever. I should have known it wouldn't be when I had to eat squishy eggs.

HAPPY BIRTHDAY, MAX!

Question: What has red hair, a sombrero on his head, and is 11 years old today?

Answer: My brother, Max.

We're at Max's favorite restaurant, Casa Taco, and he's with his favorite friends: Adam, Ben, Jared, Dylan, Brett, and Myles.

Actually, I like Casa Taco too. It's one of the few things Max and I agree on.

"Happy Birthday, Max!" Adam jumps on my brother. He takes the sombrero off of Max's head, messes up his hair, and then shoves the hat back on his head.

Max gives Adam a birthday high five.

I jump out of Adam's way. I don't want him to mess up me or my Perfect Purse, which I'm wearing tonight with the crushed velvet cover.

"Everyone, over here," says Dad. We pile into a big booth in the back corner of the restaurant.

A waitress puts a basket of tortilla chips and some menus on the table. I take a chip with one hand and hold my purse with the other. I notice my purse is the exact same color as the tablecloth.

"Look Mom, it's a perfect match," I say waving my purse in front of her face.

But Mom doesn't look at my purse. She's

busy looking at the
menu. "Who wants tacos?" she asks.

All of Max's friends raise their hands.

"What about burritos?" says Mom.

All of Max's friends keep their hands up.
But I don't raise mine.

There's nothing wrong with tacos and
burritos, but there are so many things to
pick from on the menu at Casa Taco. I like
to try something new every time I come.

Mom orders a platter of tacos and a

platter of burritos for Max and his friends. "Mallory, what would you like?" Mom hands me a menu.

I try to open it, but it's hard. One hand is busy with chips. The other hand is holding a purse. What I need is an extra hand.

"You might want to put that purse down," says the waitress. "It will be easier to read the menu."

What I *don't* want to do is put my purse down. I don't want to get anything on it. Even though I love trying new things at Casa Taco, I don't even open the menu. I can't. "I'll just have tacos," I tell the waitress.

Mom finishes ordering while Dad stands up and tells us to move in closer for a picture. I hold my purse up in front of me while Dad snaps the picture.

When I sit back down, I keep holding my purse in front of me. I also go back to eating chips. I try dipping them in salsa, but it's not so easy to dip chips while you're holding a purse in the air.

Mom looks at me kind of funny. "Mallory, why don't you put your purse down on the bench?"

Maybe Mom doesn't want to look at my purse, but someone else might want to.

I think about Mary Ann. I know she wouldn't put her purse down on the bench, and I'm not going to either. "I'm OK," I tell Mom.

Mom shrugs. "Max, why don't you open your presents while we're waiting for the food," she says.

Max nods like he loves that idea.

"Open mine first," says Dylan. He shoves a red box in Max's direction.

Max takes it and rips the paper off. "A baseball glove! Cool!" he says to Dylan.

I know Max loves it. He's been wanting a new baseball glove.

Max puts his glove on his hand. "Think I can open presents with this on?" He scoops up a small box wrapped in blue paper with his gloved hand.

"That one's from Jared and Ben and Myles and me," says Brett.

"It must be good if it's from all four of

you," says Max. He tears the wrapping off of the box.

"Wow!" says Max, staring at what he's holding in his baseball glove. "A collector's edition of baseball cards! Thanks!"

I know Max would never hug his friends, but he looks like he's thinking about it.

"Open mine," says Adam. He gives Max a red envelope.

Max takes it from him and opens it up. When he sees what's inside, he high-fives Adam with his baseball glove. "Super cool! A gift certificate to Sports World."

"You can pick out anything you want," says Adam.

Max waves the envelope in the air. "Thanks," says Max.

"Maybe you'll like what's in this envelope too," says Dad. He hands Max a yellow envelope.

Max takes it from Dad and opens it. He smiles when he sees what's inside. "Twenty-five passes to go to the batting cages!" He takes them out so his friends can see.

I know Max is happy about that present. Going to the batting cages is his favorite thing to do.

"Thanks, everybody," Max says as he looks

around the table. "My presents are totally awesome!" Then he looks at me. "Mal, don't you have something too?" he asks.

I have something. I start to give the envelope I brought to Max, but then I stop.

"C'mon!" Max sticks his hand out. "I'm sure I'll like whatever you got me."

Maybe Max is sure he'll like what I got him, but I'm not. I hand Max the card I made and watch while Max opens it. There's something inside it, but I don't know if he will like it as much as he liked his other presents.

Max takes out the card I made and reads what I wrote. But he doesn't say a word.

"What is it?" asks Ben.

"A card," says Max.

"Is there anything else?" asks Jared.

"Yeah," says Max. He turns the envelope upside down and shakes it.

When he does, something else falls out, and that something else is glitter.

Max still doesn't say a word, so I say something. "It's not just a card! It's a present card."

"A present card?" says Brett, like he has

no clue what I'm talking about.

I take the card out of Max's hand. "This is not just a regular card."

I try to explain it the way Mary Ann and I talked about it, so everyone will understand. "This card is much, much, much more. It has glitter in it, and I cut it out in the shape of a baseball, which is Max's favorite sport."

I finish explaining and wait for everyone to nod their heads like they understand the difference between a present card and a regular card, but no one looks like they do.

"Is that all you got your brother for his birthday?" asks Dylan.

"I know what you should have given him," says Adam. "You should have given him a T-shirt that says '*All I got my brother for his birthday was this stinkin' card.*'" Adam points to the card I made.

All of Max's friends laugh, like they think what Adam suggested is hilarious. But Max isn't laughing. He's just sitting there quietly.

Max almost never just sits quietly, and I don't like when he does. Especially now.

Dad looks at Max's friends, who are still laughing. "Knock it off guys," he says.

They stop laughing, but it doesn't make me feel much better.

I look at my Perfect Purse sitting on the table next to the chip basket. I think back to the wish I made at the fountain in the mall. I wished somehow, some way, I would get the Perfect Purse.

Right now, I'd like to make a different wish. I'd wish that I could magically change my purse into a birthday present for my brother.

I put my purse down beside me on the

bench. I don't feel like looking at it right now, and I don't want anyone else to see it either.

When the waitress comes to the table with the food, she asks if we're ready for the fiesta. Everyone digs into the plates of food she put on the table . . . everyone but me.

I don't touch my tacos. Mom tries to pass me the platter of burritos, but I pass on those too. At cake time, all I do is pick at my piece.

When it's time to go, Dad takes all the boys in the van. "Mallory, do you want to ride with us?" he asks.

I shake my head *no*. The last thing I ever want to do is ride in a van filled with all of Max's friends. I get in the car with Mom.

She starts driving and then looks in the

rearview mirror. "You're awfully quiet."

I shrug my shoulders and look at my purse in my lap. I don't know what to say. I know Max liked his birthday, but I feel like I didn't do anything to make it special.

"Feel like talking?" asks Mom.

I shake my head again. I feel like Mom's eyes are staring inside me. I know what she wants to talk about, but it's not a conversation I want to have. Right now, I think riding in the van with the boys would be better than sitting in the same car with Mom.

When we get home, I start to go to my room. Mom stops me and hands me an envelope. "This came for you this afternoon," she says.

"Thanks," I mumble. I take the envelope and go to my room. It's a letter from Mary Ann.

Dear Mallory,

Hi! Hi! Hi!

This is just a quickie. But I have a V.I.Q. VERY IMPORTANT QUESTION:

How do you like your purse? Have you had so much fun carrying it? Which covers have you used? Have you gotten tons of compliments? Have you used the sparkly pin yet? Isn't it cute?

I just love, love, love my Perfect Purse and I hope you do too.

If you ask me, the Perfect Purse really is perfect!

Big, happy hugs!

Mary Ann

P.S. How was Max's birthday party? Did he love his card? Did you take your purse? I bet you were the hit of the party!

I crumple up Mary Ann's letter and toss it into my trash. I pull Cheeseburger into my lap and stroke the fur on her back. "I know Mary Ann thinks the Perfect Purse is perfect," I say to my cat. "And maybe it is . . . for her."

But I'd like to give it a new name . . . the Not-So-Perfect Purse.

COUNTING SHEEP

I turn onto my right side. I roll over onto my left. I lie on my back, close my eyes, and breathe deeply. I even try counting sheep. But no matter what I do, I can't fall asleep.

I pick up Cheeseburger and go upstairs to Mom and Dad's room. "I don't feel so good," I say when I walk into their room.

Mom sits up in bed and feels my head.

"You don't have a fever," she says.

"Does your throat hurt?" asks Dad.

I touch my throat. "No," I tell Dad. "My throat doesn't hurt."

"Is your nose stuffy?" asks Mom.

I sniffle and shake my head. "My nose isn't stuffy either."

Mom and Dad look at each other. "What do you think it is?" asks Dad.

I push my stomach in a few places. "It must be my stomach," I tell my parents. "Maybe I ate too much Mexican food."

Dad shakes his head. "I doubt that's it. You barely touched your dinner. Is anything bothering you?"

I shrug my shoulders. "Nothing is bothering me."

"Usually when I can't sleep it's because I've got something on my mind," says Mom. "Maybe you've got something on your mind."

I sit down on the bed. "The only thing on my mind is going to sleep."

Dad pats me on the head. "If that's the case, you need to get back into bed." He kisses me on the forehead. "You'll be fine."

I stand up and start walking back down the stairs to my room. But I don't feel like I'll be fine, and I don't think getting back into bed will help.

I turn around and go back to my parents' room. "I guess I do have something on my mind."

Dad pats the bed. "Why don't you sit down and tell us about it."

I sit down between Mom and Dad. I look down at the bed. "I feel bad about the card I gave Max. I feel like it wasn't a very good birthday present." I wait for Mom and Dad to say something, but they don't, so I keep talking.

"I should have used some of the money I made from the salon to get him a real present."

Mom looks at me like she thinks I should have too. "Mallory, how would you have felt if Max didn't give you a present on your birthday?"

I love getting presents, especially on my birthday. "Not so good," I mumble. But there's more to it than that. I try to explain so my parents will understand.

"I wanted to get Max a present. But then Mary Ann and I had the salon and we only made enough money to buy the purse. I felt like she would be really upset if I didn't get the purse. I didn't know what to do."

"Do you think you made the right decision?" asks Mom.

I think Mom already knows my answer, but I shake my head no anyway. Even though Mom thinks I made the wrong decision, I don't want her to think it was an easy one to make.

"It was hard to make the right decision, because when I was making it, Mary Ann reminded me that Max can be really mean to me sometimes."

"I agree with Mary Ann," says Mom.

I look up at Mom. "You do?" I can't believe Mom agrees with Mary Ann. She almost never agrees with her.

"Yes," says Mom. "Max should be nicer. But two wrongs don't make a right."

"Huh?" I say. Mom's math makes no sense to me.

"What I mean is that if Max does something wrong, it's not OK for you to do something wrong too." Mom has on her teacher face. "If someone does something to you that you don't like, it doesn't make it right for you to do something they might not like back. Do you understand?"

I nod my head. "I get what you're saying." Then I stop nodding. "It's not just that I feel bad about not getting Max a present, something else is bothering me too."

Dad looks surprised. "Mallory, what is it?" he asks.

I take a deep breath. It's a lot of things, and I tell them all to Mom and Dad.

"I was really excited to get the purse, and now that I have it, it's not as great as I thought it would be. I couldn't take it to school. It wasn't fun to take it to a restaurant. I didn't get a present for Max because I got the purse instead. And Joey's upset because I haven't played with him for a long time because I've been busy trying to buy the purse.

"I was really excited to have the same purse as Mary Ann. We always like having the same things, and she loves having it, but I don't think it's been much fun."

When I finish talking, Dad starts.

"Maybe you and Mary Ann don't *always* like having the same things," says Dad.

"Maybe you just like having the same things *some* of the time. You're two different people, and you have to do what works for you."

I don't say a word, but I know what Dad says is true. He keeps talking. "As for Joey, he's a good friend. I bet if you explain things to him, he'll understand."

I nod my head. "I'm sure Joey will understand." Lately, I think he's been a better friend to me than I've been to him. I look down at my hands. "What about Max? I let Mary Ann talk me into not getting him a present, and now I feel awful about that."

Dad tilts my chin up so I'm looking him in the eyes. "Mallory, you have a brother and Mary Ann doesn't. It's probably hard for her to understand how you feel about having a brother because she's never had one."

"I never thought of that," I say to Dad.

I hang my head.

"Mallory," says Dad, "life is full of decisions. Sometimes making them is complicated. No one can make your decisions for

you. As you get older, it is up to you to make good decisions."

Even though I love getting older, there are parts of it that aren't so much fun. "I feel like I made some bad decisions and there's nothing I can do about it."

"Mallory," says Mom, "you can't take the purse back, but there are lots of nice things you can do for Max. And I'm sure you can find a way to patch things up with Joey.

Why don't you give it some thought, and I'm sure you'll come up with something."

"I'll try," I tell Mom. I scoop up Cheeseburger, kiss my parents good night, and go back downstairs to my room.

When I get into bed, I make a wish.

I wish my brain will think of something nice to do for Max and Joey.

THE PERFECT PRESENT

Some people do their best thinking in the middle of the night, and I must be one of those people. I thought of something great at exactly 3:22 a.m.

I look at my clock. Now it's 7:30 a.m. Time to put Operation *Do-Something-Nice-for-Max's-Birthday* into place.

I knock on his door and then open it

before he has a chance to tell me I can't come in. "I have something for you," I tell my brother.

"Whatever," grumbles Max.

He's been grumbling at me ever since we left Casa Taco last night.

I ignore the grumbling. "I think you're going to like it," I say as I walk into his room. I hand him an envelope with his name on it. "It's a belated birthday present."

Max rolls his eyes. "It's a card," he says like he's already gotten one card from me that wasn't so great, and he doesn't think getting a second one will be much better.

"Open it!" I tell him.

Max opens the envelope, pulls out the card, and starts reading. "This card entitles the birthday boy, Max McDonald, to one day of labor from his loving sister, Mallory McDonald."

"Not this again," groans Max. "I thought you were getting out of the girl for hire business."

I grin. "The only business I'm in is the birthday business," I tell Max. "My belated birthday present to you is that I'm going to work for you for a day, and you don't even have to hire me."

Now it's Max's turn to grin. "Great! When do we start?"

I bow to my brother, like I'm his servant. "There's no time like the present for a present!"

Max plops down in his desk chair and props his feet up on the desk. "Why don't you start with the bed."

I look at Max, then at the pile of messed up blankets. I take a deep breath. Working for him won't be easy. I pull up covers while Max sits in his chair and watches.

Then he gets up and leaves. When he comes back, he has Mom's camera in his hand. "I've got to get pictures of this." He snaps a photo of me fluffing his pillows.

When Max's bed is made, he points to the closet. "My shoes are a mess."

I look in Max's closet. His shoes are everywhere! I start picking up sneakers and looking for mates. Max takes more pictures.

When I have all his shoes lined up in pairs, Max looks at his watch. "I'm supposed to take out the trash now."

I think about all the times I've seen Max lugging those heavy bags outside. I don't really want to do this job, but I did tell Max I would work for him for a day.

I follow Max down the hall and into the kitchen. Mom and Dad are sitting at the table reading the newspaper. "Good morning, you two," says Mom.

"Good morning," I say. I reach under the sink to get a twisty tie for the garbage bag. I close up the garbage bag and start pulling the bag out of the trash can.

Dad clears his throat. "Max, isn't it your job to take out the trash?"

Max takes a bowl of grapes out of the refrigerator and sits down. He pops a grape into his mouth. "It is my job," he says, "but today, Mallory is doing my jobs." He takes a picture of me picking up the garbage bag.

Mom looks at Max like he should be doing his own jobs. "Max, what's going on? Why is Mallory doing your jobs? And why are you taking pictures of her doing them?"

"I can explain," I say. "I want to do Max's jobs."

Mom and Dad look at each other, but they look confused.

"It's a belated birthday gift," I say in my *remember-what-we-talked-about-last-night* voice.

Mom and Dad nod, like they get it. "How nice," Mom says to Max.

Max nods like he agrees and pops another grape into his mouth.

When I come back into the kitchen from taking the trash out, I pour a glass of orange juice. I drink it in one gulp.

Working for Max is a lot of . . . *work!*

"What do I do now?" I ask my brother.

"Follow me," says Max.

I walk behind him into the bathroom we share. "It's my day to clean the bathroom." Max hands me the toilet scrubber.

I guess that means it's *my* day to clean the bathroom. I look under the sink for the toilet bowl cleaner. I pour some in. While I swish it around with the scrubber, Max takes pictures.

I flush, then Max and I watch the little scrubby bubbles go down the toilet together. When the noise stops, Max looks in the bowl. "Are you ready to sweep the garage?" he asks.

"Ready as I'll ever be. But no more pictures, OK?"

Max agrees, and I head outside. When I come back inside, he gives me a handwritten list of chores.

When I'm done with everything on the list, I go into Max's room to see what else he wants me to do. But his answer surprises me. "You've done enough," he says.

I rub my ears, like maybe I didn't hear Max right. "You don't want me to do anything else?"

"Nope." Max shakes his head.

Oh no! I hope Max liked his present. "Was everything OK?" I ask.

"Everything was great," he says. Then he stretches, like he's tired. "I'm going to go lie down on my freshly made bed."

I start to go into my room, but Max stops me.

"Hey Mal," he says. "Thanks for my birthday present. I really liked it."

"You're welcome," I tell my brother. I'm glad he liked his present. Even though it was hard work, I liked giving it to him.

I go into my room and shut the door. I take a sheet of paper out of my desk.

Dear Mary Ann,
Sit down when you read this! If you read it standing, you might faint!

Today, I went to work for Max!
I know, you're probably wondering how Max got me to work for him. You're probably thinking I didn't even get paid.

But here's the part that might make you faint . . . it was my idea to work for Max, and I didn't even make him pay me.

Don't worry! I didn't eat any poisonous berries that made me go crazy. I worked for Max as a present.

I decided he needed something to go

with the card. You know how much we like it when we get something to go with the cards! Well, I decided, he would too.

And he did.

The thing is, I felt awful not getting him a birthday gift. (I know . . . how could I feel awful about anything that has to do with Max, but I did.)

Even though he can be mean to me, he's still my brother. He always gives me something on my birthday and I wanted to give him something on his.

And I'm glad I did. I could tell he liked getting a present from me.

One other thing: I know you love, love, love having the Perfect Purse, but I haven't loved having it all that much.

The Perfect Purse is really cute. But it took a lot to get it, and then once I got it, I didn't think it was that much fun to have it.

I know we always love the same things, but this time I think I loved it less than you did. I guess best friends, even lifelong ones, don't always like the same things.

Except for *Fashion Fran*. Our favorite show starts at five o'clock. Talk to you then!

Big Huge Hugs and Kisses,
Mallory

When I finish the letter, I put it in an envelope to Mary Ann and go outside to put it in the mailbox. Even though I've done a lot today, there's one more thing I need to do.

I grab something off my desk, then I walk next door to Joey's.

KNOCK, KNOCK

Knock. Knock. I knock on the Winstons' front door with one hand and keep my other hand behind my back.

"Who's there?" asks a familiar voice.

"Mallory."

Joey opens his front door and looks at me like I'm someone he hasn't seen for a long time. "Mallory who?" he asks.

"Ha, ha!" I say smiling. "Very funny."

But Joey doesn't look like he thinks it's

funny at all.

"I know I haven't been a very good friend lately," I say to him before he has a chance to say anything to me. "And I'm really sorry."

Joey is quiet, so I keep talking.

"Having the Perfect Purse isn't nearly as much fun as spending time with my friend," I say to Joey.

I look at him when I say it. Joey says OK, like everything is OK now that I've explained things. But I know Joey, and I know everything is not OK.

"I brought you something," I say to him. I give Joey what I've been holding behind my back.

He looks down at what I'm holding in front of him. "Wow!" A big smile spreads across his face. "You don't have to give me that."

"I want to," I tell him.

"But it's your favorite joke book," he says.

I look down at the book in my hand.

"Maybe you're right," I say to Joey like the idea of giving away my favorite book is really crazy. "Maybe I should keep it."

The smile on Joey's face disappears.

Then I start laughing. "Just joking!" I say. I stick the book in his hands. "Why don't you go put that in your room and get your skateboard."

The smile on Joey's face reappears. "I'll be right back," he says.

TOP SECRET PHOTOS

The only thing worse than working for Max for a day are these pictures that he took of me working for him for a day.

I am showing them to you for one reason: If you don't see these pictures of me working for Max, you will never see any other pictures of me working for Max because I am never working for him again!

You have to promise, promise, promise not to show these to anyone else!

Max's shoes smell worse than Cheeseburger's litter box!

Even the garbage smells better!

And so does the toilet!

REMEMBER: THESE ARE FOR YOUR EYES
ONLY . . . YOU PROMISED!

Some Beautiful News
By Jackson Cole

If you look around the halls of Fern Falls Elementary, you will notice that girls in Mrs. Daily's third-grade class are looking more beautiful than ever. They are wearing the latest hairstyles and the newest nail and makeup colors.

Where did they all get so fashionable, you might ask?

The answer is easy. They went to *Salon Mallory*, the newest hair salon for girls to open in Fern Falls. *Salon Mallory* is located at 17 Wish Pond Road in the room of Fern Falls Elementary third-grader, Mallory McDonald.

We had a chance to catch up with Miss McDonald following the grand opening of her salon, and here's what she had to say:

"Making money is hard work, but deciding what to do with it is even harder."

Miss McDonald wishes to thank her business partner (and lifelong best friend) Mary Ann for helping to make the salon a reality.

She also wishes to inform the public that *Salon Mallory* is temporarily closed for business. But she says if you need help with your hair, just stop by her desk at school. She's happy to give out free pointers.

We asked Miss McDonald if she has any advice for other kids starting a business. She says the

key is to find something you like
doing, and then have fun doing it.

Miss McDonald wants to wish
anyone who is thinking about
starting their own business the
best, best, best of luck!

Carolrhoda Books, Inc.
A division of Lerner Publishing Group
241 First Avenue North
Minneapolis, MN 55401 U.S.A.

Website address: www.lernerbooks.com

Library of Congress Cataloging-in-Publication Data

Friedman, Laurie B.
    In business with Mallory / by Laurie Friedman ; illustrations by Barbara Pollak.
        p.   cm.
    Summary: When Mallory's mother refuses to buy her a purse, Mallory tries a
series of businesses in order to make money and buy it herself.
    ISBN-13: 978-1-57505-925-9 (lib. bdg. : alk. paper)
    ISBN-10: 1-57505-925-8 (lib. bdg. : alk. paper)
    [1. Handbags—Fiction. 2. Moneymaking projects—Fiction.] I. Pollak, Barbara, ill.
II. Title.
PZ7.F89773Inab 2006
[Fic]—dc22   2005020620

Manufactured in the United States of America
1 2 3 4 5 6 — BP — 11 10 09 08 07 06